Fascinating Short Stories Of Kids Who Conquered Their Emotions

* * *

Dally Perry

Cover Design by
Victichy

SMARTARROW PUBLISHER

Smart Arrow Publishers

www.Dallybooks.com

Publisher's Note: This is a work of fiction. Names, characters, places, and incidents are a product of the author's imagination. Locales and public names are sometimes used for atmospheric purposes. Any resemblance to actual people, living or dead, or to businesses, companies, events, institutions, or locales is completely coincidental.

Book and cover design © 2022 By Victichy

Ordering Information: Special discounts are available on quantity purchases by corporations, associations, and others. For details, contact the publisher via email drewdallybooks@gmail.com

First Edition

ISBN 978-1-959581-10-9

Printed in the United States of America

Contents

For Valen, Vishal, and Videl.

This Fascinating Short Stories

For Kids Belongs to

Introduction

For many centuries, storytelling has been an effective approach to communicating with many others. Storytelling isn't just a way of discussing significant happenings, but a sure way to keep ourselves amused.

Storytelling builds a connection between the ones telling the stories and those listening to them. With storytelling, people get to better understand happenings that have occurred in their lives in the past. Kids aren't born with a set of vocabulary, which is a group of familiar words in an individual's language. Our vocabulary develops as we advance in age. It's a useful tool in helping us to communicate better and gain more knowledge.

Storytelling helps to improve children's expression a lot better. They can identify their emotions, know what to do with the various kinds of emotions they feel, and better articulate their thoughts and experiences.

Research has it that storytelling is effective for children who are guided successfully in languages that require them to be successful in communicating their emotions and accepting the emotions of others. Storytelling helps to build emotional literacy. It also helps to build the child's vocabulary and social-emotional development.

*
*
*
*

2

ATTITUDE

Not Everything Is Black Or White

Narrowmindedness is destructive

When George was in elementary school, he got into a serious argument with another boy in his class. This event taught him a great lesson he will never forget in a hurry.

George was sure that he was the right one and the other boy was wrong. On the other hand, the other boy was very much convinced that George was wrong and he was the right one.

So their teacher decided to step in and solve the issue. She brought them both to the front of the class and put each of the boys on each end of her desk. The teacher placed a big round object in the middle of the desk. She asked the other boy first, "What color is the object?" The boy said, "Black." George was livid. How can this little fellow say that the object is black when everyone can see that it is white? Even a blind man can see that it is white. He couldn't contain himself and another argument ensued immediately on the color of the object.

The teacher told George to go and stand where the other boy stood before and told the boy to stand where George was before. Then she asked George what the color of the large object was. George answered and said, "White!" It was an object with two differently colored sides. So from George's former viewpoint, the large object was white, while to the other boy, it was black.

From that very day, George stopped arguing without putting himself in the other person's shoes. He started looking at the challenge through the eyes of the other person to fully comprehend their point of view. Being narrow-minded is destructive.

The Poorest Man With Just Enough

Happiness is dependent on what you think and not what you own

A long time ago, there lived a family who lived in a little country home. They were the average kind of family, but they were content with what they had. The family had a strong bond that was the envy of their neighbors. It was a healthy bond everyone needs to covet.

One fateful evening, the family gathered to have dinner as one big family, which was their usual tradition. Then there was a knock heard at their door. The father stood up to go check who was behind the door. As he opened it, he saw an advanced man in rags who looked unpleasant and also smelled the same.

The elderly man was carrying a full basket of tomatoes. He only came by to ask if the family would like to buy some of his tomatoes. The family bought some quickly, as their dinner was getting cold.

In no time, the family became friends with the old man. He would come by weekly to sell tomatoes, spinach, onions, and many other edible vegetables, and the family would buy them off him. The family discovered that the elderly man was almost blind due to cataracts that were clogging his eyes, but still, they enjoyed his company and would miss him anytime he didn't come as he usually would.

One day he went out to sell more of his vegetables and he stopped by a friendly family and recounted how someone dropped some clothes in a basket for him at the front of his door. The kind family was glad that now he has new sets of clothes. But the old man said, "I am happy I could find a family who needed them and I gave them all out."

The kind family stood and watched in amazement as to what kind of being the old man was.

Love At First Lick

Every dog has its day

During the summer holidays, Frank volunteered at the vet so he could be close to the dogs. His favorite of the dogs was the dog they called Bobby. It was a funny-looking dog because of its appearance and by far the funniest-looking dog Frank had ever come across all his life. He loved dogs so much. Any dog breed was great for him. He never segregated or had a special breed in mind, and dogs were just his first love.

Bobby had thin curly hair that didn't cover the whole of her body, and some of her skin was exposed due to the lack of hair, which made her look like a sausage without enough toppings that were applied sparingly. Bobby's eyes bugged out like she was constantly surprised and her tail was like that of a rat – thin and long.

Bobby was abandoned by her owner. That's why she didn't look so good. She had suffered neglect and her owners just got tired and brought her to the vet as they didn't want anything to do with her ever again. The vet held Bobby and tried to put her to sleep. Within seconds, Frank saw that Bobby had a beautiful personality, even though her looks betrayed her.

The vet sterilized Bobby and injected her with all that was needed at the time. Frank then advertised her in the local newspaper with the caption: "Funny-looking dog, well mannered, needs a loving family." Soon, a teenage boy called in, wanting Bobby, but Frank warned that Bobby was a dog with unusual looks. The teenager told Frank that his grandfather's eighteen-year-old dog just died and they need Bobby at all costs. Frank agreed to give Bobby to this family, so he gave Bobby a warm bath, brushed her scanty fur, and got her ready to meet her new family (at least Frank prayed they were the loving and caring family needed for Bobby).

Soon they arrived in an old-looking car and they parked in front of the vet. Three kids jumped almost at the same time for the door.

They picked Bobby up in the most loving way into their arms and brought her to their grandfather, who came with them. They placed Bobby in their grandfather's arms as he patiently waited in the car. Frank accompanied them to their car to observe Bobby's reaction to this family.

In the car, the grandfather rocked Bobby like a baby. He stroked her scanty hair while Bobby licked his face and she wagged her tail in so much excitement that Frank was shocked. Bobby acted as though she had met this old man before. The connection was extreme, and this was love at first sight at play. The elderly man said that Bobby was perfect and that they would take her.

Frank was happy that Bobby got a better family to call home, well deserving and worthy. On a closer look, Frank discovered that the grandfather couldn't see. He had a milky film covering over his eyes, so it was love at first lick for the duo; not love at first sight.

Just Frederick Is Perfect

Your present circumstance doesn't define you

During the early part of September, the weather was cold. It was the kind of weather to wear an extra sweatshirt for.. Coach Nate was a soccer coach who worked with kindergarteners and first-graders. On this particular day, it was the first day of practice. Children dressed in double sweatshirts were present. They also wore gloves, jackets, and mittens.

Coach Nate sat the kids down on the dugout bench. Since they were meeting each other for the first time, Coach Nate asked them all to introduce themselves so that everyone could get to know each other.

Each child went up and down the benches a few times, with each child mentioning his or her name and the names of the other kids sitting to the left and to the right.

Coach Nate decided to test the kids' memories and their level of paying attention after they have done the above exercise for some minutes. He asked for a volunteer who could name all the names of the other eleven kids on the team right there in the presence of the teammates.

A brave seven-year-old boy named Jason stood up to the challenge. The challenge was for him to go up to the left side of the bench and begin to name each child's name and then shake their hands and move on to the next child. Jason began well, while coach Nate stood behind observing with keen eyes. Jason went down the row – Emmanuel, Ben, Peter, Sophia, Matilda, Frederick... on getting to Frederick, Jason stammered out Frederick's name and stretched out his hands to shake, but Frederick didn't extend his hand. Everyone looked at Frederick and took turns to look at each other, wondering what in the world was happening. Frederick just sat there with his hands tucked underneath his jacket.

Coach Nate asked, "Frederick, why won't you allow Jason to shake your hand?" Frederick still sat put. He looked up at Jason and then at the coach, but said nothing still.

Coach Nate asked, "Frederick, is anything the matter?" Frederick looked up to him and said, "Coach, I don't have a hand!" Frederick unzipped his jacket and to all their amazement, his arm stopped at his elbow. There were no fingers, no forearm, and no hand.

For some seconds Coach Nate couldn't utter a word. He was shocked and displeased with himself for pushing the poor boy that much just for him to reveal his weak arm. While still trying to figure out how to approach the situation, the other little kids gathered around Frederick, bombarding him with questions about his arm in the most pleasant and sincerely concerned way.

One of the kids asked, "Frederick, what happened to your arm?" Another asked, "Does it hurt Frederick?"

By now, Frederick had taken off his jacket to show his new friends what they all wanted to see. They all stood in awe and shock at what they beheld.

After a while of taking a long look at Frederick's arm, he told them all in a collected and calm way that he had always been like this and that there was nothing special about him because of it. He then turned to coach Nate and said, "Coach, I don't want to be treated differently from the other kids, so please treat me like everybody else."

From that day on, things changed for Frederick. He was treated differently, just the way he wanted. Frederick was no longer a kid with one arm, but he was simply Frederick, one of the other players on the team.

Children are far more than just tiny people. They are special people and there aren't any other beings like them in the world.

The Connection In The Flood

Humanity isn't lost

Alexis woke up to the sound of thunder and the unintentional rhythm of rain that flogged the earth, which frightened her to her bones. It was 2:25 a.m. and the sound of thunder kept crashing in at intervals in the loudest of volumes. Alexis wasn't alarmed at the thunderstorm. Soon she went back to sleep. Alexis was awoken by his parent's shout at 6:12 a.m. as they bombarded his room.

"Alexis! Alexis! Wake up! Our home is flooding!" Alexis was still very grumpy and tossed around in bed, but his dad nudged him persistently on his shoulders until he was wide awake. Alexis got up with a jerk and ran downstairs with his pajamas. It was a dreadful sight. The water from the flood rose six inches high. The water was cold and he was freezing. His parents and he started taking what they could save from the flood all the way upstairs.

Alexis's parents were beyond angry. Just within an hour, the flood had risen to eighteen inches high. It was getting worse. Every single thing was moved to the first floor: the computer system, and the big smart television and huge boxes filled with their most valuable possessions. Their sofa, piano, Persian rug, laundry machine, water heater, dryer, and furnace weren't saved. They all were destroyed by the flood.

Alexis's father went to the basement after they smelt a terrible odor oozing from the water close to their bathroom. Their toilet downstairs seemed like a faulty geyser. It had water gushing out of its bowl at maximum speed. Dad rushed upstairs to call on neighbors but their lines weren't going through. Alexis's mom pushed through the flood over to their neighbors but she reported that they couldn't do anything either.

Right before their eyes, their home was getting destroyed, and they couldn't do a thing about it. It was hard to take in, and they all felt terrible and helpless. That was a sickening feeling of complete hopelessness.

The front porch was the only outlet to leave their home. The water kept rising outside as well. Now the water was close to five inches away from their front door. Alexis's mom told him to pack a quick bag with his clothes and valuable items. With this instruction, Alexis knew what was happening. He immediately packed a few of his clothes, stereo, CDs, a few books to read, puzzle games, and baseball cards.

Alexis's mom packed her china dishes and rolled up the Persian rug that she could save and kept them all upstairs. His dad could only pack up some clothes. He was very frantic and irritated that the rain came to ruin his hard work. The situation was very horrible. When the family was ready to leave, the water had made its way into the front door. Out on the street, were rafts floating around in the deep water, now rising up to six feet.

Much later, it was safe to come outside after the rain stopped, and the community learned that the National Weather Service had earlier announced that there was going to be a flash flood, but many didn't know. Many of the neighbors gathered outside at one corner of the street, all of them counting their losses and those who lost more than the others began to compare those with the greatest loss. It was a time to bond as everyone shared similar pain at the moment, and everyone comforted each other. Neighbors became friends and friends turned into family. The suffering brought them together as one.

Alexis and his family had to stay at their friend's house, where they ate, took their baths, did their laundry, and bonded. The flood taught Alexis a hard lesson. Through the flood, he learned what true friendship meant and how a family is important. He learned to value what he had and to better empathize with those in their low estate and feel pure compassion for them and not compelled sympathy. Alexis also learned that connection is key to all of humanity

Taming Chelsea's Wild Emotions & Insecurities

Don't hide behind your insecurities

When Chelsea was in junior high school, he was so mindful of what his friends thought of him. Chelsea was much taller than his friends in his grade and this particular factor made him very uncomfortable. Chelsea decided to walk around with those who scorned others and make unfriendly jokes about other kids in school, just so that the attention was shifted from him due to his rare height.

Chelsea pulled various hurtful and harmful pranks on the other kids just to hide behind his own insecurities. One day, just before gym class, Chelsea and his friends put a hot and peppery substance in the gym shorts of one of the kids on the basketball team. The player was so embarrassed and ended up in the nurse's office for treatment. It wasn't funny like he had thought it would be, especially to Chelsea's father, when he learned of the pain his sin caused another child.

Chelsea's parents never thought that his behavior was funny and they warned him about it so that he'd change. His parents talked to him about the golden rule in which he should treat others the way he'd love to be treated himself. Chelsea's parents disciplined him severely about the way he treated others. In harming the other children, Chelsea destroyed his own reputation and made him into someone who shouldn't be looked up to. Chelsea's mean friends looked up to him just because he was tall. That was the only factor that made him superior. Nothing more. They thought of him as a confident tall boy who took laws into his hands, but deep inside, Chelsea was a frightened little boy who didn't understand himself and one who had no control or grasp of his emotions. The emotions he felt ran wild in different directions without any technique to tame them.

Chelsea's parents desired that he become a leader with an exemplary life, one who was decent and could impact others with his own life. His parents taught him to set goals and be the best he could be in everything he set his mind to do. Chelsea's father reiterated to him anytime he had the opportunity to talk with him that he should strive to be the leader he was meant to be, be a big man at heart, in his actions, and his body as well.

Chelsea had questioned himself whether it was imperative to be the type of leader his father wanted him to turn out to be which he believes is resident inside of him.

Chelsea had to direct his energy to be the version of himself by focusing on basketball, and then he became a leader in the game. Chelsea took his responsibility to make a good example of himself to the world to heart. He would often stop to think before doing anything. He became more intentional with everything he did. He made some mistakes, because we are all humans after all, but he learned from them.

To date, Chelsea changed for the better. He still seeks opportunities to make a difference in his world and to make himself a good example following his father's advice. Now, dear reader, it's your turn to affect the world positively – be that leader you would be proud of. Let people have a good enough reason to look up to you.

Keep Up The Good Work

Maintain a positive attitude

Gary's first season of playing basketball began when he turned ten. He used to shoot hoops before he turned ten. He had always loved to play basketball from a very tender age. Gary had separated parents, he had a basketball at his dad's and his mum's place, and this makes it easy for him to practice at both their houses anytime he was at either of theirs for the weekend, or holiday, or whatever the case may be.

Gary would ask his mum to drop him over at the gym before basketball practice began. He loved basketball so much that it was all he spoke about. He lived to meet with his teammates and the basketball drills were much fun for him. Many times, Gary loved to stay back at the gym to keep shooting the basket long after practice was over, but his mom would always drag him out of there so he could at least rest and eat something.

Gary and his mom had the most beautiful talks when he had the time to talk about something else other than basketball. One evening, Gary said he needed better basketball shoes, as the ones he had were wearing out. His mom heard him right and clear but she didn't have the means at the time to replace his shoes. She looked at the one that was wearing out, but it still looked just fine.

The first game of the season had come and the gym was filled to the brim. Gary was elated because his team – the Hornets – were on fire, and more so because his dad was in the stand just a few feet from him. Gary had a determined look as he joined his teammates. The game began but Gary was on the bench; he watched as his other teammates were running round and round on the court. By the fourth quarter, the Hornets had won the game and Gary hadn't even touched the ball.

The games that ensued were kind of the same. The team kept winning, but still, Gary hadn't touched the ball. When he was later given a chance, he ran so hard on the court, but when he got the ball, he quickly threw it to a teammate. While his parents watched the match, they sat with their hearts pounding against their chests.

After the game, Gary's mom asked him, "Gary, do you still enjoy playing basketball?" Gary answered and said, "I love basketball very much. But I do know that some of the kids play better than myself, so most times when I am opportune to get the ball, I just get to throw it to them."

In the following days, Gary's mom ran into an old friend of hers who used to play basketball when they were much younger. She expressed how Gary loved the game, but wasn't doing so well at it at the moment, but that he desired to be better.

Her friend asked her if Gary had good shoes and she hesitated before responding. Her friend knew that they needed to get Gary new basketball shoes. So they both went shoe shopping for Gary's shoes. They got Gary a beautiful high-quality basketball shoe. Gary was very thankful to his mom and prayed that his new shoes would help him win the preceding games.

Gary's unrelenting enthusiasm and devotion to basketball ran by quickly and Gary still felt he was not the best player on his team, but that was fine because as long as he loved the game, he was content. Gary continued to work very hard and practiced even harder each passing day. As time went on, he improved. He wasn't discouraged again. His new shoes seemed to have raised his confidence level up a notch and he thanked his mom the more first his new shoes. Gary told his mom more descriptively about the new plays he thought of and how proud he was to be part of such a prestigious basketball team that never loses.

The Hornets made it to the playoffs. Gary scored eight points at the end of a very interesting game in the presence of a standing-room-only crowd. When the season came to a close, it was time to award the best players for the season. Gary began to guess who would take the award of best defense, most valuable player, most improved, and best all-around player. Gary's team came second in that season and all the teammates got a trophy each. Close to the end of the award ceremony, the Director stood up, thanked all that were present, and then said they weren't done awarding yet.

The director said there was one last award left, a very special award for a special team player. The director said that this player shows up for each game with a positive attitude regardless of the present circumstances he was in.

He never argued with his referee or other players, had never been late, and never missed a practice or a game. He knew his place while playing, and his teammates spoke highly of him. He played for the love of the game, and he always ran hard and tried his best. "So, the Sportsmanship Award for the season goes to Gary Solomon!"

Immediately, the whole attention was on Gary. His teammates and friends were congratulating him and gave him high-fives and soft slaps on the back. Gary's eyes were filled with tears. Just a few yards from him were his parents with tears in their eyes as well. His father smiled back at him while his mom blew him several kisses.

With the ovation still high in the hall, Gary stood up and walked over to the director to claim his trophy, the second one at that. Gary got the most impressive award that night. Gary was so proud of himself and was glad he didn't give up when the chips were down. He thought to himself that now that he had two awards, one would be at his mom's and the other at his dad's.

The Navy Blue Boots

Don't compromise yourself. Be proud of your gift.

Phil woke up this morning especially excited because of the lovely poem he had written about his mom. It was a Monday morning, and he is prepared to hit the ground running regarding every school work that he will encounter today. Phil wore his strong navy blue boots to school on that day, which was his first day in school.

It was the poetry festival day, and he was elated. At Phil's former school, he won the poetry ribbon annually. Phil sucked at sports, but he thrived in poetry.

Phil was ready to share the poem he wrote for his mom at the poetry festival. He was excited to share how special the poem was to him to his fellow fifth graders and his teacher, Mrs. Nuel. To Phil, the poetry period was stretching too long and he became anxious and dehydrated as his throat got dry. When Mrs. Noel announced the next class which was the poetry class, Phil felt accomplished when his name was mentioned to render his poem. Phil cleared his throat, took a deep breath, and began to recite his poem without looking at the sheet because he had internalized the words, perfected the rhymes, and counted the beats several days ago.

Phil had only gotten to the third verse when his teacher Mrs. Noel stopped him with fury spread all over her face. Phil stopped, wondering what wrong he had committed and waited for her to say what wrong he had done.

Mrs. Noel said, "Phil you were supposed to write an original and read it to the class and not another person's work! What you are doing is plagiarism and that's a serious offense!" Phil tried to explain to his teacher that he was reciting an original he wrote for his mom and he wasn't reciting another person's work. But his teacher wasn't having any of that, in fact, in the class one of the students said out loud when Phil said the poem was an original saying, "Yeah, right, who do you want to fool?" The other children giggled.

Phil felt like he was falling from a high building and was stuck mid-air and then landed in a stream without water. He was flabbergasted. His mouth was open but couldn't utter any words. How could his original be questioned this badly? He even tried to explain, but wasn't given the chance

Phil was sent out of the class to never return until he apologized for lying that that piece was his. Phil left the classroom to stand outside. He wondered what just happened to him. Phil stood out there for over thirty minutes with his mind running wild back and forth until the school's janitor came to ask him why he had stood outside of his classroom for that long.

Phil and the janitor became friends one morning before school commenced. When he saw Phil sitting alone, the janitor invited him to help open up the classrooms and they got talking. From that day onwards, that seemed to be Phil's job, while the janitor would continue his other duties like wiping the chalkboards, mopping the ground, wiping the surfaces, and turning on the heat. That particular morning, the janitor was speaking to Phil about Mark Twain who said that the difference between the right word and the almost right word is like the difference between lightning and a lightning bug. Phil loved that. His mom would have loved it as well.

The janitor asked Phil again what had happened that he was sent out of his classroom. He waited for Phil to answer, and he looked so kind and sympathetic that Phil told him the entire event that transpired while he fought hard not to cry.

The janitor heard it all and asked Phil what he wanted to do about the situation as he frowned his face, and he jerked an enormous yellow duster out of the pocket of his gray overalls and rolled up the duster into a tight ball.

Phil told the janitor that he didn't know what he wanted to do with a helpless shrug. The janitor told him, "But you are not going to stand here all day, are you?"

Phil said, "I guess I'll just do what she said – I'll apologize and tell her that I am sorry.

The janitor said, "You'll apologize? Apologize for what, exactly? Apologize for your own work?" Phil nodded his head, saying, "There is nothing else I can do, and she has refused to give me a listening ear. It's really not a big deal. I guess I'll just stop writing anything this good in her class ever again."

The janitor looked at Phil, utterly disappointed by his response, but Phil disregarded the janitor's look and shrugged and went his way back to where he stood earlier. The janitor followed after Phil, his tone stern and reassuring, saying, "Phil, admitting defeat when you are supposed to stand up for yourself is a very dangerous habit, believe me when I say so!" His eyes peered into that of Phil's, unflinching. Phil blinked and looked the other way, but the janitor's eyes followed his, and they both caught Phil's clean navy blue boots.

The janitor's face changed from a frown into a smile. He laughed softly and told Phil, "You'll be fine, just fine. I won't have to worry about you. When you wore those boots this morning to school, you knew exactly that you were the only Phil Brigham in the whole world."

The janitor dropped his duster and put it back into his pocket and pointed at Phil's boots with a big smile, saying, "Those are the boots of one who is strong enough to take care of himself and knows when something is worth fighting for."

Those words stirred something inside Phil that had been resting for too long since he was admitted into this school, and then he knew the right thing to do. With his direction restored, he took a deep breath, knocked on his classroom door, more coordinated, and prepared to face Mrs. Noel, reciting his original poem to the entire class, come what may.

No Excuse For Poor Grades

Cherish your wins

Josh was finally fifteen years old. He had waited for this year so long that it seemed like an eternity before it came. Josh was elated and felt more responsible all of a sudden. He felt that he was growing into a man and a lot dependent on him to accomplish in his family. He would have loved to spend the day with his dear friends, but it was snowing and the weather wasn't so favorable for an outing, so Josh used that opportunity to clean out his room of junk and trash a lot of kid stuff (apparently he wasn't a kid anymore).

When Josh was done, he had four big garbage bags to take out, and then he wondered how he had been living in the room with so much trash, with three bags of dirt and one bag of toys and other children's stuff. Josh decided to take the first bag out. While dragging it down the staircase, a picture dropped to the ground. It was an image of his friend Paul. Paul was Josh's friend from fourth grade. They would have still been great friends if his father wasn't transferred to Budapest to be a vice president of a big bank.

Paul was the most intelligent boy Josh had ever known. He always got straight A's, looked geeky, had freckles, and was handsome at the same time. A part of Josh desired to dislike him, but he just couldn't bring himself to do so. Paul was equally nice. Josh envied him and desired to be like Paul with every fiber of his being.

Paul's hair was the color of honey. He had short curls like corkscrew curls, and they often bounced when he walked. Josh's hair was straight and wispy. Paul was a little plump, while Josh was tall and skinny. Paul had dimples on each side of his mouth that made him appear like he was smiling at all times. For Josh to smile, his grandmother had to call him "funny face" before he could break into a grin. Josh wasn't the smiling type. His folks didn't understand why his face was that serious. His mom advised him to stand in front of the mirror and practice how to smile, for at least ten minutes daily. It was a concern to her. Josh tried it a few times and got tired of trying. He thought he looked dumb to be learning how to smile, so he just stopped entirely.

Paul was an honor student and got to sit in the front of the class. Josh's desk was at the back, on the side of the room where there were no windows. Paul was a perfect reader who never stumbled or slurred words, but Josh wasn't and their teacher wasn't pleased with him for not being as smart as his friend Paul. The teacher was always correcting Josh too soon anytime he read. He was never given a chance to say the words, and didn't seem to believe in himself, unlike how he believed in Paul. Josh thought to himself that if only his teacher had faith in him, he could do better.

One good day after soccer practice, Paul and Josh stood together, waiting for their mothers. All of the other kids' parents had come for their wards except for them. Paul rested on one of the stone columns that braced the wrought-iron gate in front of the school, while Josh rested on the other side of the gate, watching Paul read his book. By this time, they weren't friends yet. Paul noticed Josh was looking at him and then he asked in a kind and calm voice, "What are you looking at?"

"You," Josh said, unable to stop staring.

"Why?" Paul asked.

"Because you look like you are very sad," Josh said. Josh's mother's advice kept ringing in his head that it was rude to stare, but he kept staring nonetheless.

Josh said, sounding like he had made a huge blunder that was so grave, "I got a B+ on the history test." Josh asked, almost upset, "Is that why you are sad?" Josh wondered, what in the world is wrong with a B+? It didn't make any sense to Josh.

Josh told Paul, "B+ is not the end of the world, you know. I would love to have your kind of grades, I'd love to read and spell like you, and have the teachers dote on me — and you are here sulking over a B+? You must be over entitled!

Paul looked at Josh, knowing he had no idea what he was going through, so he came closer to Josh and whispered into his ears saying, "Can you keep my secret?" as though they were already close friends. He said further, "Promise me you won't tell a soul. Promise me."

The fact that Paul wanted to share his secret made Josh feel good, and important, like the popular kids he rolled with. Josh was more surprised when Paul grabbed his arm tight while he was waiting for him to promise to keep his secret safe. "Promise me," Paul requested again. Josh then said, "I promise." Then Paul released Josh's arm.

Paul whispered very low to Josh with tears already flowing down his eyes, saying, "My dad beats me with a leather strap. Straight A's are all he wants to see. I have to get straight A's." Now Josh got the clear picture, and he felt so sorry for Paul and wondered what kind of a father could do that.

Josh asked Paul, "You mean your dad will beat you because you got a B+ instead of an A?" "Yes," Paul cried, hanging his head as if he was embarrassed to show his face. "He will beat me again tonight, immediately after he returns from work and sees my history result!"

"He hits you?" Josh asked again, not wanting to believe him, not wanting to believe a father would do a thing like this or be so wicked. Paul replied, "Yes. My dad says I have no excuse for poor grades. When he was in school, he always had straight A's, and since I'm his son, I must do the same."

Josh asked, "Where is your mother when your dad is hitting you?" Paul responded, "She leaves the room until my dad is done beating me. When he is gone, she comes in to hug me and tell me how my dad loves me and how all he is doing is for my good." Paul continued shrugging his shoulders, "Besides, it only hurts for a little while." Josh told Paul, "My dad says my brother and I must have a good education. Every day after returning from school, we're not permitted to play outside or have friends over until all of our homework is done. My father is pretty strict about that, and he isn't happy when we come back home with poor grades. But he never ever hits us."

Paul asked surprisingly, "So he doesn't punish you when you make mistakes?" Josh said, "Well, not exactly. Not in the manner in which your dad does." Paul asked Josh, "What do you mean?"

Josh responded saying, "Well, if you knew my dad, you'd understand. All my dad will do is stand straight as an arrow, his hazel eyes fixed on yours (don't even think of trying to break eye contact with him). Then, in a very low and stern voice, my dad will slowly call out your first name. Then he will say your middle name in the same slow and stern manner in which he did your first name. And that's all he will do. Trust me, my brother and I know he means business."

"And then what?" Paul inquired with fear in her eyes and shiver in his voice, expecting to hear a dreadful tale of a gruesome sentence much worse than being flogged with a leather strap.

"And then what?" Paul asked again, expecting the worst!

Josh responded, "Then we fix the problem quickly, we work harder when we have another opportunity to prove ourselves worthy again, and do a better job."

Just ahead, Paul's mom was circling down the driveway towards them to come to pick up her son in a big, gray car. Paul said to Josh as he dashed toward the car, "That's my mom. I have to go now. Don't forget Josh, you promised me."

Josh nodded in affirmation and watched Paul get into the passenger seat at the front. "Bye Paul," Josh managed to say before the car cruised off. Paul and Josh became the best of friends from that day forward, and Josh never had to envy Paul ever again.

ANGER

How Often Do You Get Angry?

Anger affects you spiritually

One day, a humble disciple named Kwang asked his Master, "Master, is there any way to measure my spiritual growth?" The Master answered and said, "Of course, there are numerous ways to do that." Kwang asked his master to give him one.

The master said to Kwang, "Note how many times you get emotionally angry during the course of the day. Keep a record of it. As the figure keeps going down, then you are ready to begin your walk to your spiritual growth."

Spiritual strength can be evaluated on the foundation of the wisdom of the mind. A spiritually strong individual does not struggle, he doesn't go through pain or suffer defeat, he recognizes that the supreme in the inside of him is what guides him in all that he does, and for that reason, he cannot lose, but experience joy all year round.

Kennedy And The Stranger That Brought Him Peace

Overcome Your Anger

Kennedy had a rough life. He woke up one day and had a very angry temper. Everyone knew he was struggling in life. His wife left him and took the children with her. Everything about his business nose-dived, he lost his friends, and many family members withdrew from him.

Kennedy used anger as a weapon over people, and he always got away with it. But one day he ran out of luck. He met a man on his way home named Nathan and he vented his anger on him. To Kennedy's amazement, Nathan seemed to see above Kennedy's anger and into him. Nathan then told Kennedy in a quiet voice, "You do not need to be scared. Just let the world see and know that true you that is hidden behind this angry mask you have come to own."

Kennedy's countenance dropped. He became peaceful and became calm all of a sudden. He went away that day a changed person, Nathan noticed that he had been putting up a front all this while just to hide his weakness, and that showed he had better stored inside of him.

Kennedy wondered how a total stranger saw through him that bad, and even advised him to let go of all his fears and drop anger altogether.

Kids and teenagers can get upset and fight an adult, but no one is scared of a child's anger. The honest reason is that children are vulnerable and helpless while adults are physically superior to children. An adult has little expectations from children who display anger and are less disappointed with anything because they don't have mastery of certain emotions just yet.

If Kennedy had reached out to those who love him to express his innermost feelings, it would have helped to address them earlier. But Kennedy bottled up a lot of things and that made him employ "anger" as a tool to shield himself and wade off any form of attention from those who love him and care for him genuinely.

When we feel angry, it is good to express how we feel in a sane way. Don't throw things in the air, break things, or harm ourselves or others. Pass across the message of how you feel sensibly so that the point is driven home. Anger isn't a bad emotion when it is channeled for the greater good. So children, be angry but use it for good.

Will's Close Call

Put your emotions in check no matter the circumstance surrounding it

Some years ago, Will's mom visited the doctor because of her neck. In recent times it had gotten swollen a little bit and needed the doctor's attention again. The doctor told Will's mom she needed to visit a hematologist immediately. The doctor told her that there was something up with her lymph glands, and she needs to have a biopsy done. Will's mom was slated to have this surgery on the 5th of June.

When Will found out about the date scheduled for his mom's surgery, he got very upset and screamed that that very day was his birthday. He begged that his mom move the date but she told him that she tried and the doctor told her that was the available date and how the urgent surgery was needed to salvage the situation of her declining health.

Will yelled, crying, "I hate you, Mom!" and ran into his room and locked the door. Back in Will's room, he sat down, wondering why the most terrible of things always happened to him. He wondered what he had done to deserve such an unfortunate life! Will didn't for a second think of his mom who was the one who would go under the knife. He didn't console her in any way. All his thoughts were selfish thoughts of his birthday that had been ruined by his wicked mother who put her surgery date on his birthday.

Will went about, angry and sulking for the remaining part of the weeks preceding his birthday. Will knew he acted in a very selfish manner and shouldn't have acted that way, but still, he did and he did nothing to change the narrative. Will's actions were hurting his mom the more and everyone could see how miserable she was becoming by the day. Will knew it wasn't his mother's fault, but someone had to be blamed and Will made her the one to carry that heavy burden.

Fast forward to Will's birthday. His parents left early for the hospital and his aunt came around to babysit his little brother and watch over him. There was a picnic in the yard for Will. He had lots of presents from friends and played so much with his friends. But in the midst of it all, there was a strong restraint that everyone was just pretending to have fun. The tension was real and they weren't having fun. How can they even have fun when their family member was under the knife battling for her life, while they acted like they were having fun at Will's party? But Will felt it wasn't fair. It was his birthday for Christ's sake. All the attention should be on him and everything on earth should be suspended for him to be celebrated.

Later that night, Will's parents returned very late. His mum had a bandage around her neck, rested her neck on her husband's shoulder, and could barely talk. Will's dad explained how they suffered to get home. They had a bad tire that took hours to change due to the bad weather while his mom stayed in severe pain in the cold car.

Will's mom still managed to call Will to her room. She pulled out a bag and handed it to Will. It was his birthday present, a

Walkman. She apologized for not having it wrapped. She managed to have these few words pass her vocal cords. Will's mom further said, "Sorry we didn't have time to get you some batteries, but we'll get them soon, not to worry." All Will could say was, "Thank you!" he took the gift and left his mom's room.

Some weeks after the surgery, the doctor called to say that Will's mom had cancer. Will became quiet and withdrawn. How could he have been so insensitive to his mom? He thought about how he acted and the things he said that he couldn't take back. He felt sick to his stomach. Memories of his dad's cousin being diagnosed with cancer hung in the air, and in a few months, he had died. That was his favorite uncle, and this loss hit him hard. He wondered what life would be like to lose his mom, and then he went to apologize for his insensitive behavior and the cruel words he used. They forgave him and promised him that everything would be fine.

A few weeks after, Will learned that the doctor had dismissed his mom from the cancer threat, that he read his mom's case inaccurately and that she would be fine. Will was beyond excited.

He ran to his mom's room where she was resting to hug her for a long time, until he fell asleep beside her.

Will was scared to his bones to know that he almost lost his mom to cancer like he did his uncle. He promised never to behave badly again, or be selfish. It made sense that you really don't know the value of a thing until it is no longer available.

The Bobsledder's Jacket And The Little Good Samaritan

Attitudes are self-created

For so long, Jerry had longed to be in the Olympics. For many years, he had worked very hard to become a great bobsledder (that's an individual who participates in bobsled\toboggan\ snow tubing).

He had practiced and trained so hard that he could be a better bobsledder. On this fateful day, Jerry and his colleagues traveled for the Winter Olympics to Sapporo, Japan as the American bobsled team. On their way to the opening parade, other athletes from all over the world gathered there to march into the Olympic stadium.

Jerry and his colleagues were joyful and ecstatic. Everything was perfect and this is what they had been praying for all their lives.

Everything was perfect, except for Jerry's torn Olympic jacket that got ruined when he climbed a fence the previous day. The American bobsled team jacket had in front "USA" and behind "Olympic rings." Jerry knew his jacket was torn but he felt no one would notice that it was.

His friend Nelly said to him, "Jerry, they will notice it. The Japanese people notice everything, especially things like that!" Jerry didn't answer Nelly. Nelly's father was murdered by the Japanese in the island battles during World War II. Since then, Nelly has always felt uneasy about anything Japanese, worse still that they were present in Japan. He had his guard up 24/7.

Out of nowhere, a little Japanese girl came by and pointed at Jerry's torn jacket sleeve. Jerry just smiled back at her and waved at her. As she kept poking at his torn jacket saying things he didn't understand, he said, "Good morning," so the young girl could leave him be, and turned to his friends saying, "I don't know what she wants from me, I can't understand a thing she is talking about."

The Japanese girl was a beautiful cheeky girl with long black straight hair. She kept smiling back at Jerry and saying things, but unfortunately, none of the American boys understood her. The little girl started tugging at his jacket, and then she started removing her coat while she looked up at him. Then Jerry's friend said, "She wants you to remove your jacket!"

So Jerry took off his jacket, and handed it over to the little girl, saying, "Oh you want to try it on? Sure kid, here you go." The little Japanese girl collected Jerry's jacket and took a bow. He took a bow as well. On raising his head, he saw the little Japanese girl running off with his jacket. He screamed, "Hey!" "Come back here now!" while chasing after her. Nelly shouted after them both with so much hate in his voice, saying, "Thief, little thief! She is stealing the jacket! I told you these people are not to be trusted, I told you, Jerry, I told you!"

Not long after, a crowd had gathered and the little girl was nowhere to be found. One of the American boys who came along with Jerry for the bobsledders shouted at Nelly, saying, "Quiet

Nelly! Someone who understands English might hear you!" So, Nelly kept quiet, but he was very furious by now.

Jerry was very worried and said, "What do I do now? I can't play without my jacket. What can I do now?" His teammates told him he will have to play without his jacket.

Twenty-five minutes later, they were standing with the other American athletes, waiting to start. Nelly stood by Jerry and he could sense that Jack was troubled. Nelly told him that it was okay and they were with him. Nelly wished he could get hold of that little Japanese girl and teach her a quick lesson she would never forget in a hurry.

Unexpectedly, Jerry felt a pulling on his shirt sleeve. He looked down. Guess what? It was the little Japanese girl. "You ran off with my jacket, where in the world did you go!" Jerry exclaimed, and he held her on the shoulders so she couldn't run off. The Japanese girl only smiled at him and held out Jerry's jacket to him. Jerry took it and in an instant, he understood. The huge tear in the sleeve of the jacket was no more. The Japanese girl had taken his jacket to go and quickly amend it, and he was here hating on her. The jacket was so professionally sewn that he couldn't see a loose thread hanging out of any corner. Jerry held it up very close to himself to be able to see the stitches on the jacket.

At this point, Nelly's mouth was agape while he stared at the little Japanese girl. The Japanese girl smiled at both of them again and took a bow again. Nelly then said in shock, "She didn't steal it! She took it to get it fixed!" Another bobsledder said, "She must have gone to her mother or someone and had it fixed quickly because they didn't want you embarrassed at the parade! This is amazing Jerry!"

The music began and the parade started. In the streets of Sapporo, thousands of athletes marched as one, proudly wearing the colors of their countries with great honor. Each walking with the same gait, same rhythm, and the same joy, each of them resolute to be the best that he or she could be.

On the parade ground was an extra marcher on that glorious and proud day. Two Japanese girls are on the shoulders of two

American bobsledders named Jerry and Nelly. These Japanese little girls spoke no English but they were English at heart.

LOVE IS A FORCE

Love Me, Love My Dog!

Let love lead

One time, there was a freshly married couple who were so much in love with one another. They desired that their love would increase and never decrease. So, they went to a Master and inquired, "What can we do to make our love stand?" The Master responded, "Love other things collectively."

The same applies to normal friendships. Challenges arise when both parties are not in sync with the same likes, interests, and wants. This is not to say that you have to love what your partner or friend loves, but if the dissimilarities in the above factors are huge, your relationship might suffer. Develop a liking for what they love, and open your mind to understanding them more. The idea is that the dislikes shouldn't outweigh the likes we see in the

other person.

There Is No Greater Gift Than True Love

Love sacrificially

A long time ago in the beautiful town of Memphis, there lived a boy and a girl who were so in love with each other. The boy was called Tobi while the girl was called Antonia. This duo did everything together, there wasn't a time when each of them didn't know about the whereabouts of the other person; they hung out together, visited recreational sites together, and celebrated many occasions together with great joy.

Soon, it was time for Christmas, and while they were both too poor to give each other a gift, they decided to do something to change the narrative. All the boy had was a wristwatch with a strap that had worn out while all the girl had was her precious golden hair. So, Antonia sold her golden hair to buy a new strap for Tobi's worn-out strap, while Tobi sold his only dear possession which was the watch to buy Antonia two combs for her beautiful long golden hair. When Christmas came, they exchanged their gifts and laughed hard at the irony of life which was – there wasn't any watch for the new strap and no hair for the comb.

This story shows us that love is a great gift. See how Tobi and Antonia sold out their most prized possession for love's sake? Their display of love was priceless. Yes, a worldly gift is great, but there is no greater gift than true love.

Is It Love Or Ritual

Let your love stand the test of time

Frederick met Helen and their chemistry was off the hook. They fell in love and decided to get married. They were so happy and their public display of affection encouraged others old enough to be married to leap.

With time, this favorite couple bore a son and they called him Henry. Henry brought more joy to the couple, until one day. Out of nowhere, their love turned sour. They began to quarrel about the pettiest things and their marriage began to suffer. One day, their son Henry asked his mum Helen, "What are the things people say to each other when they get married?" Helen lovingly responded to her son and said, "Couples getting married will promise to love each other and be kind to each other for the rest of their lives."

Henry thought for a minute and said, "Then you and dad are not always married, right?" Helen was dumbfounded at her son's sincere response.

Many people tend to forget their vows when the going gets tough in marriage and in other relationships in life. Vows that are supposed to be scary are not taken for what it's worth anymore, instead of doing things just as a common ritual, we should love and mean it.

Love Tames The Rebellious Mind

Love above rituals

There was once a very rigid man. He wouldn't eat or drink during the day. Everyone honored the man and reverenced him as a holy and disciplined man. In fact, the prosperity of the town was attributed to his constant praying and fasting. It appeared that the heavens approved of his ways, so a bright star beamed above a nearby hill, noticeable by all to see during the day, but no one knew how the star got there.

One day, the man chose to go up the mountain. A little village girl was bent on going along with him and he obliged her. On that very day, the weather was hot, and as they climbed up the mountain, they got thirsty. They kept going and going and they got very thirsty. The man told the child to drink, but she refused and said she would only if the man would drink the water first. He was in a big fix now, right in front of him was a dehydrated child, but she was too stubborn to drink, because she knew when the sky was bright, he wouldn't like to eat or drink.

As they went on, dragging the matter back and forth, the man decided to drink the water and eat so that the child's suffering could end. He did that for the sake of the child. He became downcast as they journeyed and did not want to look up at the sky in fear that the star up the hill would have disappeared. But when he finally looked up in the sky, to his amazement the star that was formerly one was now two.

The moral of this story is that, while we perform rituals or do things that are for the good of everybody, we tame the rebellious mind. Whatever religion you belong to, the sole aim is to love, love another wholeheartedly and completely.

FORGIVENESS IS KEY

From Thieves To Disciples Of A Monastery

Learn to let go easily

Some college dropouts sought a way to make quick money, so they started to steal little things, and in no time they took it up a notch and started stealing valuable/big things. One time, they robbed a monastery. They got away with everything in it. As they were leaving, the head of the monastery stood in their way with a bag in his hand. The criminals thought that had been apprehended and would be handed over to the law enforcement agents in the land. The elderly man told the thieves with a bag in hand, "You left this bag behind, you can go along with it as well if it pleases you." The thieves sensed the monastery's sheer sincerity and felt bad for their action. They then turned away from their evil ways and became disciples of the monastery.

Forgiveness triumphs over every Tom, Dick, and Harry. The value of forgiveness needs to be nurtured meticulously, for it is the virtue of everyone who will go very far in life.

"Because Mum Said Nothing!"

No pointing fingers, learn to forgive others

Austin and his mom were washing the dishes one Sunday afternoon, while his father and younger sister were in the living room watching their favorite show on the TV. Out of nowhere, there was a loud crash of plates breaking and everyone went silent. The father and daughter in the living room decided who must have dropped the plates out of the two that remained in the kitchen. The girl said, "It has to be mum that dropped the plates." Her dad said, "How did you get to know that it is mum when the both of us were in the living room together?"

The girl replied to her dad saying, "Because mom didn't say anything!" Many times, we are quick to raise fingers against others when we too make silly mistakes once in a while. We have to consider that we all are human and we err. This way, we all should learn to let go easily and develop the culture of not putting others down when they err.

Most Popular Prisoner With A Forgiving Heart

Love comes naturally than hate

James Gregory received a call in the wee hours of the morning, which was a very odd time to call. As he picked up the receiver, it was the voice of a heartless policeman who rudely informed him that his son was dead with no explanations whatsoever or condolence expressed, just a brief order summoning him to the police station.

James Gregory's son was twenty three years old before he died. His name was Brent Gregory. One evening he was coming back home with his friends after a nice evening in Cape Town when he had an accident as he drove, climbing the hill at speed in his little Toyota and then ending up behind a semi-truck that was packed by the roadside. This accident had the better part of James Gregory who has always been a good man. The accident led to depression and extreme grief. James Gregory blamed himself greatly and he was on the verge of losing his purpose and enthusiasm in life. Soon, he lost his faith in God. No one was successful at comforting him, and he no longer made sense of the world. No words could help ease his aching heart. How do you pull through after losing a dear child? James Gregory was lost in extreme grief. He rudely chased away ministers, family, and friends who gathered in his house for his son's burial, and he didn't remember that he had done that the next day.

A brief condolence note came in for James Gregory, neatly addressed by the only man on earth who truly understood the grief he was experiencing at the moment. He was also summoned by the person who wrote the letter. James left his place of work, which he resumed just to forget the anguish he was going through. He got to the author's house and the man couldn't find the words to say to his dear friend, so he led James by the hand into the garden they often strolled in.

They walked in silence for a while until they got to the tree they often sat by because of its shade. James' friend told him, "It has happened and it is a terrible thing. Let's recall the good times we both had with Brent. He was a brilliant boy and I have photographs of him sitting here by the tree, reading his Bible, and discussing bible passages with me. He was caring and loving, and in situations like this, that's a value so rare."

James' friend talked about their common pain. He said that "Time will heal physical wounds/inflicted wounds, but time will not heal the invisible wounds. Individuals will mean the best when they speak these kind words to you, but they won't know. It is vital to note that they mean these words even though they cannot feel them."

For the first time since he lost his son, these were the words that comforted him. James knew that those words came from his friend's heart, which was once broken as he is now. Twenty years ago he lost his own son – Thembi, who was also twenty-three years old at the time. Thembi died in a car accident, as did Brent

Gregory. It was James Gregory that delivered the ill news to his friend, who desired to mourn alone. He had stood all through the night, with no food and no sleep. He couldn't cry or talk. He stared out the window at the night sky.

James Gregory came back the next day to check on his grieving friend and asked if he still wished to be left to grieve alone. His friend answered and said, "No, please stay with me." A few days later, James Gregory came bearing more bad news that his friend had been denied the right to go attend his son's funeral.

It was a piece of difficult news to break, but James had to tell it regardless, as it was his job. James Gregory was a jailer and his friend, Nelson Mandela, was his prisoner...

Nelson Mandela believed that "nobody is born hating another being for the color of his skin, or his background, or his religion. People need to learn to hate, and as long as they can learn the act of hating, he believes they can equally learn to love, for love comes more naturally to the human heart than hate."

Nelson Mandela taught James Gregory the pure act of love above hate. James Gregory loved Nelson Mandela and the impact he brought into his life to this very day. Nelson Mandela's only crime was to stand up against racial hatred in South Africa. He was imprisoned for fighting a just cause and he forgave the people who hurt him badly because he believed that hate was a greater burden to carry on your shoulder, unlike the compelling nature of the heart, which is love.

Rolihlahla Mandela was born on the 18th of July 1918, in a little town close to Umtata in the black homeland of Transkei. The English interpretation of Rolihlahla is, "troublemaker." Rolihlahla's father – Henry Mandela – was a chief counselor to the chief of the Thembu people. Rolihlahla's great-grandfather was a Thembu king. Rolihlahla was given the name Nelson by his teacher on his initial day of elementary school to honor the memory of Lord Nelson.

Growing up, Nelson learned a lot from his father and at the Thembu court of his ancestors, Xhosa warriors, with their long history of protecting their motherland from European invaders. All of these formed a path and inspired Nelson to free his own people from the suppressive white rule.

Nelson Mandela became a lawyer in Johannesburg. He observed the clear discrimination amongst the white South Africans of English descent, from the Dutch settlers who struggled for South Africa's independence from the hands of England, and then the black South Africans, who were often denied their fundamental human rights. Things got worse for the black South Africans in 1948, when the Apartheid system was imposed by the Afrikaners' National Party when they assumed power. It upheld segregation and separation at its peak.

In apartheid, blacks were enforced to reside in selected neighborhoods, and then were later forcefully moved to extremely poor black homes. They attended very inferior schools. Universities that were formerly for all races were now forbidden for blacks. Most times, the black South Africans were made to feel as though they were a lesser form of a human, and that was exactly how the leaders of the National Party viewed them. A black South African, or a "kaffir," as they were often called, meaning "nigger," was a term often used by the Afrikaner extremist. To the Afrikaner extremist, a kaffir didn't possess the inalienable right to be among the living. The killing of blacks wasn't a big deal nor was it a grave crime to many Afrikaners of the time. The lives of Kaffir were taken away for a little as being bold enough to confront the ills of the Afrikaners or mere talking boldly to a white man. Apartheid was just a legalized form of hatred.

Nelson Mandela's fight against injustice led to his first arrest in 1952, when he spearheaded the Defiance Campaign, which was a mass protest against apartheid. He was charged and put away for violating the Suppression of Communism Act, given a suspended sentence, and banned from attending any public gathering or leaving Johannesburg for the month. All through the 1950s, Nelson Mandela was often arrested, jailed and released, and banned from public activities.

In 1960, the African National Congress (ANC) was banned after the anti-apartheid protestors in the black township of Sharpeville staged a huge rally in opposition to the passed laws that restricted where blacks could travel in South Africa, and where over sixty people were killed by the South African police. Since that occurred, the ANC abandoned its nonviolent approach to emancipation and formed an armed wing of resistance with the uMkhonto we Sizwe (Spear of the Nation), or MK. Nelson Mandela was its leader.

Nelson Mandela went under while still organizing armed resistance. His victory, and the failure of the authorities to apprehend him, got him the title the "Black Pimpernel." In 1961, he fled South Africa and journeyed throughout Africa and Europe in search of support for the MK, and physical training for MK guerrillas. He returned the following year and was apprehended, tried, and imprisoned on Robben Island.

He was returned to Johannesburg in 1963 to stand trial for high treason and sabotage along with other ANC leaders who were equally arrested in Rivonia, a thriving Johannesburg suburb. Nelson Mandela's closing remark when he was being tried by an all-white judicial system turns out to be one of the most celebrated speeches in modern political rhetoric: "I have fought against white domination, and I have fought against black domination. I have cherished the ideal of a democratic and free society in which all persons live together in harmony and with equal opportunities. It is an ideal that I hope to live for and achieve. But if needs be, it is an ideal for which I am prepared to die."

Nelson and the other accused were sentenced to life imprisonment and sent to the harsh conditions of Robben Island. In 1990, it was twenty-seven years of living in the most gruesome conditions, but he was given the freedom to live in the country he had fought for and was ready to die for. In 1993, Nelson Mandela became the first democratically elected South African president. Today, South Africa turned out to be the land Nelson Mandela dreamt it would be.

Nelson grew to love his jailer, who happened to be an agent of the government who tormented him. He chose to forgive him and see him as first a human and then a man. He didn't see him for his color, but for his decency that earned him so much respect from Nelson and great friendship. Nelson's approach made James Gregory respect Nelson Mandela a great deal and knew that he was wrong to have believed that he was an enemy of the state.

Nelson preached that love comes more naturally to the human heart than hatred. Even though Nelson Mandela is no more today, we cannot forget his forgiving spirit to the country he loved, and how his sacrifice, dedication, and undisputable dignity released South Africa into the strong arms of love it had been aching to reside in.

KINDNESS

The Lesson From The Stray Dog

Don't pay evil for evil

One day, Michael strolled down the street with his dog. Out of nowhere, three people showed up from their homes and blocked Michael's way and that of his dog. The first man screamed at Michael, saying that his dog chased his cat to a tree. The second man yelled that Michael's dog bothered him all through the night with his continuous barking. The third man said that Michael wasn't feeding his dog well. Michael responded to the three men in a calm voice that stunned them all, saying, "Do you derive joy in being so unkind to people? This dog sensed how kind I was and he kept following me. He is not my dog, he is just a stray who fell in love with me and me with him." When foolish people attack you meaninglessly, as long as you are innocent, you can enlighten them with your show of kindness.

Making Room For Humanity

Good people still exist

Once upon a time, there was a famous saint called, Felix Peterson, who was popular for his large-heartedness and kind heart. Felix Peterson toiled hard for the poor and did all that he could to ease the life of others and make their life so much better off. Felix would, most times, go on long strenuous tours just to get contributions for the less privileged.

One day, while he was out begging for alms for the needy and neglected, a man who Felix asked for money for his course spat in his face, but Felix said politely. "Thank you, Sir, that was mine, do you have anything for the poor?"

The world lives on because of blessed souls like Felix Peterson who devote their lives to the service of others.

Words Cut Deep

Speak compassionately

At the doctor's office, none of the appointments were on time, so the crowd kept increasing in the doctor's waiting room. An elderly man stood up and walked to the receptionist, asking, "Ma'am, my appointment was for 8 a.m. It's 10 a.m. already and I cannot afford to wait for too long. Can you kindly give me another closer appointment?"

A man in the crowd who heard the old man's request said, "What is the urgency about? This man is just in his sixties, so why the rush with his age?" The old man heard his remark and looked back at the lady smiling, saying, "I am seventy-nine years old, and I am not in my sixties." We all need to be kind to everyone around us, there is no excuse for speaking harshly or inconsiderably to others just to be heard or just to feel better about ourselves. It is also important to note that time is more precious to the old as they get

closer to the end of their lives. They have more sense of urgency

and they should be spoken to kindly.

The Dying Man That Saved His Helper

Be merciful

One day, an extreme Eastern Christian ascetic was walking up a mountain road in Tibet. A Tibetan monk journeyed with him. The two travelers knew that a storm was growing and they had to reach their destination before it got dark or they would die in the shrill mountain cold.

As they rushed onward in the icy breeze, they went by a cliff from which they heard a groaning voice. At the foot of it was a man who had fallen. He was badly hurt and wasn't able to move. The Tibetan said, "In my conviction, right here is karma. This is the work of fate, the effect of a cause. This dying man's doom is to die here, while I must continue on my journey which is for a greater cause." But the Christian answered, "All you've said is against my belief, I must lend a hand to my brother and come to his aid." On hearing this, the Tibetan rushed away to continue his journey while the Christian man descended down the slope, carried the man on his back, and fought his way back up to the road that was very dark now.

The weight of the dying man was increasing, and the bad weather wasn't helping. The body of the Christian man was dripping with sweat, and then he tripped over an obstacle and fell to the ground with the dying man he carried on his back. He was overwhelmed with pity and bewildered. Close by was the Tibetan he had journeyed with from the beginning. He was frozen to death and the Christian narrowly escaped it because he showed kindness to a total stranger. The Christian's body was kept warm because of the strenuous exercise he engaged in by carrying the injured man on his back. That way, he kept warm all through the journey.

It is good to show kindness to those in need, no matter the circumstances they find themselves in. We all serve others in various magnitudes, be it intentional or not. We all can nurture ourselves to render fruits of kindness in all we do daily, and soon it will become our lifestyle and we can change the poor kindness

ratio to something fair.

Chin Up

Live in the moment

One time, there lived a clock repairer. He often went from one house to the other, fixing broken clocks and watches. At some point, as he was set to fix the pendulum of yet another damaged clock, to his amazement, the clock spoke to him, pleading and saying, "I beg of you, Sir, please leave me alone. Show me this rare act of kindness on your part. Reflect on the number of times I will have to tick per minute, then an hour, then during the day, and in the coming years." The clock repairer answered wisely, "Try not to think about the future. Just do your best tick, one at a time, and you will enjoy every tick for the rest of your life." And then the clock took the repairer's advice and decided to live and enjoy each and every moment of his life. To date, it still ticks with joy.

Our current moment will not be agonizing if we live fully in it. It is torture to have your body in a place at 8 a.m. and your mind in that same place at 5 p.m. You have to be living in your present realities. Enough with the regrets and mistakes of the past. It is a good thing that you acknowledge that you made a mistake, leave it all behind, and make new and fresh realities.

You failing at your school work doesn't make you a failure. Remaining and grieving over the failures of the past is what makes you a failure. So move past it already, the future holds better things in store for you. Chin up!

JOY

Mount Delight

Choose happiness

Henry was always depressed. Nothing seemed to cheer him up. One time, a friend of his told him of an energizing aromatic plant that grew on top of a place called Mount Delight. Henry wasn't certain of its location, so he studied a map and went looking for the mount. As Henry mounted, he came in contact with a hiker who tried to talk him out of climbing any further. The miserable man disputed why he shouldn't be allowed to climb a mountain for a very potent herb that guarantees bloom, strength and power. To this, the climber responded, "Mount Delight is not here. You have to look for it in your heart."

People often like to look for joy outside of themselves and they end up getting frustrated. Happiness is a state of mind that can be gotten by nurturing a peaceful mind, and by living a good life. You can intentionally choose to live a happy life. It is within your control.

Make Someone Laugh Today

Laughter is potent medicine for the soul

A long time ago, there was an Englishman who was popular for his sense of humor and wit and many people knew him for this particular reason. He died and went to Heaven. He felt very nervous. The Englishman didn't feel he had so many good deeds in the world. Just ahead of him was a long queue, so he watched and listened to the others get judged right in front of him. While they consulted their huge book, God said to the first man in the queue, "I can see here that I was hungry and you fed me, you are a good man. Come with me my child, let us go up to Heaven!"

The second man's turn reached to be judged. He did a good deed and was ushered into heaven because he gave water to the needy when they were thirsty, and that was a good deed worthy of a sure pass into heaven.

It got to the third man, the man had gone to visit him at the hospital when he was very ill, and so he was sent over to Heaven for his good deed. And so it went on... The Englishman now sat observing his sense of right and wrong and felt he had so much to be scared for. He had never given food or drink to anyone ever before, he has never visited the sick nor has he gone out of his way to lend a helping hand to the less-privileged.

When it was the Englishman's turn to be judged, God said he had used his jokes to help the discouraged and depressed feel better. God said his jokes were always timely and the funny stories he shared had also made him laugh and be happy too. So God sent the Englishman to heaven for his very good deed.

It's good to laugh and share jokes when you can. Laughter conveys happiness and good health. In this manner, people who promote and exercise humor and wits help the whole of mankind.

HUMILITY

So Much To Learn

Confess your illiteracy with humility

The illustrious Duval, the librarian of Francis I, was seen as a very intelligent and well-educated man. Sooner or later, a self-centered man who was jealous of the librarian inquired several disrespectful questions of him and Duval responded, saying that he didn't know. The egoistic man got upset at the librarian and told him how disappointed he was that the librarian ought to know, because the Emperor pays Duval for his knowledge.

Duval said, "The Emperor only pays me for the things I know. If he were going to pay me for the thing that I do not know, all the riches of the whole empire would not be enough."

Duval, though being well-educated and vast, didn't condemn the man who reprimanded him for not knowing the answer to a question he asked, he simply admitted that he didn't know all things. Only a wise man can maintain such a level of humility in the place of abundant knowledge.

The Rare Game Of Chess

Humility brings you before kings and queens

One afternoon, Queen Elizabeth II of the United Kingdom rang the bell for one of her servants. He did not show up and so she rang again and again, but still, he didn't come. When she got tired, she walked into the servant's room and saw him busy playing a game of chess. He was neck deep, his full concentration was in the game, so he missed the bell that rang multiple times.

On seeing the queen, everyone present got up quickly and bowed to her. The servants were still on their knees when she drew a seat closer to the chess table and looked sternly at the chess board for the next possible move and then played. The next thing she said was, "And who was playing?" The opponent who was playing jumped to his feet and affirmed he was the one. The queen ordered him to sit down to everyone's amazement.

Then she instructed the servant she had been ringing all the while to go run the errand she was calling him for and promised him that she would win the game in his favor.

The queen displayed a rare form of humility that was never heard of ever before. A great man is known if he is humble or not. If you desire greatness, then you have to begin by serving others. Pride will not take you anywhere, but humility will take you to the top and beyond.

Sleep On The Floor

Humility is an antidote for relieving stress, tension, worries, and loss

of sleep.

A long time ago, a banker lost so much fortune and was feeling miserable and wasn't in a very good place. He made attempts to work on his mood in order to be a happy man again, but all he tried didn't work, and he seemed to be drowning even more.

Many of his family members tried to help, but all they did was a total waste of their time. Soon, he found a monastery during one of his many wanderings and searched for peace of mind. As he walked into the monastery, he found others there meditating, but he was too disturbed to bring himself to even meditate.

He wondered how he could come into a monastery and still feel hopeless when a few seconds ago he felt as though all his prayers would be answered. It was certain that the distraught man wasn't getting peace of mind at the monastery, and so he stood to leave, even more disappointed and dissatisfied.

When he left, the Master said an ironic statement, "Persons who sleep on the floor, will on no occasion fall down from their beds." 'Sleep on the floor' – this speaks of improving the quality of your humility. There is no sense of hurt with humility. Loss of worldly gain will hurt your ego. The banker lost his wealth he had stacked up for years. That might not have been a huge loss for him, but in the eyes of the public, his position was lowered and his status in society would be questioned going forward. The bigger one's ego gets, the greater would be the downfall of the individual. Cultivate humility and there will never be any cause for stress, worries, tension, and lack of sleep.

HEALING FROM LOSS, GRIEF, HURT, AND BITTERNESS

Time Heals All Wounds

Allow time to do its work, then healing is assured

Dr. Logan was a celebrated writer. Piper Kerman was his dedicated biographer. One time, Piper Kerman was greatly insulted by one of her contacts and she felt very bad that she would be treated in that manner. So, she took the issue burning in her heart to Dr. Logan and reported the whole thing to him.

Dr. Logan advised Piper to consider how inconsequential this matter that hurt her so much would be in the next year from now. She gave it a quick thought and felt more at peace knowing that she had just been overworking herself for something she could just simply let go of.

Nothing stays forever on planet earth. Time evens out a lot of things, and it is the best healer. Within the course of time, once excruciating pain will no longer exist.

Miles The Just And Upright Man

Hurt is inevitable, build a tough heart

Once upon a time, there lived a man named Miles. Miles was a very loving, just, supportive, and upright young man, and everyone loved him for being just that.

Miles would go above and beyond just to lend a helping hand to people. All he wanted was for them to feel better and smile that their issues had been solved and there was absolutely nothing to worry about anymore. Miles often did these things at the detriment of his own needs, just so that we all are happy at the end of the day. Many people profited from Miles' kindness, but he was often taken for granted.

Soon, Miles realized that he had been used by many to whom he had been generous, and he became depressed about this awareness. Miles learned that the Buddha was passing by his village and made up his mind to tell him all he felt. Miles asked the Buddha, "In your opinion, what do you think I should do to people as a form of revenge for them taking me for granted and using me after every good thing I did for them?" To this, the Buddha replied, saying, "Miles, get more virtuous than they are."

From this, Mile understood that he didn't have to stop being kind to others, but he wouldn't care anymore what people say behind him, nor would he care if he was being taken for granted – because he loved to help people and not being of service depressed him. So Miles could also choose who he helped going forward, for he had the prerogative to do so.

We don't have control over how others behave towards us, but we have full control as to how we react to it. People will continue to act the way they please, but that shouldn't change who we really are. We must surmount the feelings of bitterness. We can also develop our virtuous nature. The more upright we get, it makes the job easier to control negative emotions.

Pay No Attention To The Noise

Meditation is the absence of self where hurt cannot reside

A long time ago, a Master kept wrestling a brick against the ground close to where his disciples sat meditating.

In the beginning, the disciples were okay with what their master was doing, as they felt it was a way to test their power of concentration, but in no time the noise became unbearable and irritating and one of the disciples exclaimed, saying, "What under the heavens are you doing Master? Can't you see I am in meditation?"

Then his Master replied, saying, "I am trying to polish this brick to make a mirror from it." The disciple said to his Master, "You must be going crazy! How in the world does one make a mirror out of a brick?"

Then the Master replied, saying, "I am no crazier than you! How can you make a meditator out of the self?" Since it is an impossible task to make mirrors from bricks, it is the same way it is impossible to meditate in front of self. True meditation is being dead to self. If the surrounding noise is getting you upset, then your meditation journey is still far off.

The reason for meditation, ironically, is to learn to be without purpose. When we engage in this life, we have to have a goal, purpose, dream, and aspiration in mind.

Most of our actions are basically a means to an end, which points us repeatedly to a future that isn't in existence. With meditation, when no goal interrupts it, we then find the wealth and wisdom of the present moment we are living in. Then we start to know the phenomenal things that are resident in each and every one of us, not what will be or might be when we think of events of the past – but what we are!

CONCLUSION

As Kids we are faced with different types of emotions every days of our lives. We have to learn to control and master our emotions. Because we alone have the key to our happiness. "You got to train your mind to be stronger than your emotions or else you'll lose yourself every time."

"You may not be able to control every situation and its outcome, but you can control your attitude and how you deal with it."

Made in the USA
Monee, IL
29 November 2022

18858968R00066